Praise for *The Tid*

"I LOVED this stunᵢ books, the writing is beautiful and haunting, immediately sweeps us away, this time into the dark and mysterious world of the tide singers" **JENNIFER KILLICK**

"A stunning intertwining of Welsh folklore and gripping adventure ... This is a one-of-a-kind story of the wild unknown" **KATE HEAP, SCOPE FOR THE IMAGINATION**

"A captivating fantasy with an important message for us all" **EDSPIRE**

"A chillingly good story for Upper Key Stage Two" **JUST IMAGINE**

"Wonderfully moody and atmospheric ... Williams' compelling storytelling and Ro's moody illustrations deliver an unforgettable read" **A WORD ABOUT BOOKS**

"With an enticing brew of magic, loyalty and fighting for what's right, *The Tide Singer* is great to read aloud or in groups. Mysterious, atmospheric and highly readable, this clever modern myth is perfectly pitched to KS2 readers who need a high-interest, fast-moving text for a small group reading or book clubs" **SCHOOL READING LIST**

"Every time I read an [Eloise Williams] book, I declare it to be my favourite. Then I read another and decide I have another favourite. I LOVED this strange, beautiful tale!" **REBECCA F. JOHN**

"Has the distinct feel of a classic ... I can't recommend this book highly enough" JULIA THUM

"Williams skilfully weaves an evocative tale – adventure mixed with myth and dark mystery. The setting, the weather, the mystical girl all add to an atmosphere steeped in old-world legend. A fascinating read ..." AN AWFULLY BIG BLOG ADVENTURE

"Enthralling for anyone. Myth meets historical fiction in this haunting drama" JAMES HADDELL

"This was amazing, just so amazing ... It was eerie, it was clever and unique ... I've never read anything quite like this" A PAPER GIRL A PAPER TOWN

"An original and mesmerising story full of folklore, music and a real appreciation for nature. Wonderful words perfectly complimented by stunning illustrations from August Ro" RHIAN TRACEY

"A lovely story of the power of the sea. And next time I collect some sea glass I will think about the singers in the sea and their tears" STEPHANIE COATES

"This is an incredible book. I loved every minute of it ... It is Eloise at her best, with evocative storytelling and fabulous imagery ... Another must-read" NESS HARBOUR

The CURIO COLLECTORS

Eloise Williams

Illustrated by
ANNA SHEPETA

Barrington Stoke

First published in 2023 in Great Britain by
Barrington Stoke Ltd
18 Walker Street, Edinburgh, EH3 7LP

www.barringtonstoke.co.uk

A CIP catalogue record for this book is available
from the British Library upon request

ISBN: 978-1-80090-200-8

Printed by Hussar Books, Poland

For my own Ma

CHAPTER 1

1896 – Digswell Water

The day is simmering hot, and Ma Hawker has sent us to the riverbank to search for curios. Sometimes we find things that have been carried downstream. We take them back to the caravan, clean them and put them on display.

Tom is knee-high in the water, watching a fish swimming around his shins. I am paddling at the edge. The sun is high in the sky, so bright I can't look at it even with my hand shading my eyes. The river glitters, sunlight dancing on its wobbling surface.

"Tom, help me find things," I say as I scan the mud of the bank for anything useful. "Tom!"

I shout his name this time because Tom is in a world of his own.

"I *am* helping," Tom replies. "I'm searching with my feet."

He demonstrates by stepping forward and wriggling his toes about. Then he loses his

balance and falls in, getting a mouthful of water. Tom spits it up like a whale from its spout (I saw this once in a book). We laugh until we cry.

It's delightful to be here where the blue kingfishers dart past and herons swallow eels in one long gulp. It's almost impossible to worry about anything. Almost.

I want to take a rest, but Ma Hawker says we need to find more breath-taking curios to draw people in and make money. Each time we get to a new town, we put on a show. Ma displays our curio collection and tells made-up stories about how and where she found them.

People are happy to pay for a thrilling tale of adventure, and Ma is very good at it. I'm an apprentice storyteller, but while I'm learning, my job is to bang a drum to get a good crowd together. Meanwhile, Tom goes about collecting money in a hat from the audience.

Sometimes we even sell the curios to rich people. Ma hopes to make enough money to travel the world one day. We want to go with her.

We've been following the river for a few months, stopping to make camp in various places. Since we arrived here, we've found a ring made from a spoon, coins, a doll with its head missing and an otter's skull. I found a chamber pot last week and chased Tom with it, trying to put it on his head for a joke.

But today, the river is shallow and stubborn and brings us nothing. I hold my hair up to cool the back of my neck. I hear the taps of a far-off woodpecker busy at work. A bee drones close to my ear.

I search again. Something glints, mostly hidden by the mud. I paddle over, then claw it out with my fingers. Tom sees I have found something and comes to look. It's a blue poison bottle in the shape of a coffin. Not very interesting, but better than nothing.

Our caravan sits just beyond where the river bends, and we begin to wander back. Tom points out every colour, bird and tree, and I listen cheerfully.

Winnie, our horse, is wearing one of Ma Hawker's old hats. Her ears poke through holes we made in it. Winnie munches happily at the sweet warm grass, her tail swishing away flies. Tom goes to her, and I climb onto the roof of the caravan, where Ma Hawker is smoking a pipe.

She's not our real ma. We don't have one. When Ma Hawker took us in, we became the Hawkers. Like a real family. Once she told us that she was a hundred years old. Once she said she was from the moon.

"Ma, we found something," I say.

Ma puts her hand out to inspect our find. I give it to her shyly, wishing we'd had better luck. Her fingers swiftly rub away the dirt, and she sniffs at the bottle to see if there is any poison left.

"Is it any good, Ma?" I say, my voice small. One day I'll discover treasure, but not today.

"Everything is useful," Ma says, and smiles. She puts her arm around me. "Well done, Lily. Can you check on the soup for me?"

I clamber down from the roof and put the bottle into one of the storage cases we've fixed to the outside of the caravan. Ma gives a long sigh. We are in trouble, that much is certain.

The pot hangs over the smouldering fire. I pump air into its base with a pair of bellows to get flames. Then I dunk the ladle in the soup but find mostly just watery stock. I spy a few lonely carrots.

My skin prickles. I should be able to sort this out and get us more food. I'm twelve, Ma Hawker is ancient, and Tom is only ten. He is making Winnie stare at the sky and explaining to her how he would paint it if he had the chance. My eyes water, and I tell myself it's the smoke.

Ma fetches bowls, and I spoon out the soup, giving Ma and Tom all the carrots and keeping none for myself. We sit on stumps I cut from a fallen tree when we first arrived and slurp and slap our lips together.

The weather is cooling as the sun lowers, and sparks from the fire wriggle upwards in tiny red lines. Ma breaks hunks of bread. A hopeful crow lands close by, but she shoos it away when normally she would share.

Tom gulps down his food, then stares at his empty bowl. Ma goes off to the bushes, and I pass him half my soup. I haven't the stomach for it.

I throw a bit of bread to the crow and watch it take flight with the food in its beak. We like crows. They are wise and clever, and Ma says they know everything.

Dusk gathers, turning the sky to orange and pinks, thickening fast to indigo. Night bleeds in, and the sky soon glitters with stars. When it gets too cold, we wrap up in shawls and I throw a blanket over Winnie, kissing her velvety muzzle goodnight. She nuzzles me with affection.

By the time I get inside, Ma has put Tom into our bed already – his eyelids droop sleepily. I squeeze in beside him, snuggling up for warmth. Ma sits with a candle lit, practising her reading a while. Then she licks her thumb and finger and snuffs the candle out. She sits next to us to sleep.

I listen to a hunting owl, foxes howling and the soft trickle of the river. The noises cover the grumble of my stomach as I desperately hope that tomorrow we'll find something good so we can buy more food.

CHAPTER 2

The morning sunshine pours in the window. Tom has most of the blankets, and Ma is singing loudly and tunelessly outside. She juggles three eggs, her face wrinkled with concentration.

Licking my lips, I take our kettle down to the river to fill it so that we can boil the eggs over the fire. We eat, the three of us, chattering our way into the day.

I finish repairs to the wheel of our caravan. It won't last for ever, but it will have to do for now. Tom draws a kestrel with a bit of charcoal from last night's fire. Ma mends the dress she's wearing, sometimes pricking her leg with the needle.

I go to gather more wood to keep the fire going. We've been in this spot for a fortnight now, making long overdue repairs to the caravan and our curios. It's the longest we've stopped in one place for ages, so I know my way about.

It's fifteen paces in bare feet to the willow. From there you need boots to protect your feet from being stabbed by sticks. I take the smell of woodsmoke with me, wrapped in my clothes, into a world of rippling green. This feels like a happy day.

I'm the first to hear the farmer's whistle. We are under strict instructions to tell Ma if we notice him coming. I run back to the caravan, and birds shriek in alarm. Ma is not at the fire.

"Tom," I say, beckoning to him.

Tom knows the rules well enough, so drops his paper and runs up the wooden steps to the caravan ahead of me.

"It's the farmer, Ma," Tom calls.

We rush inside. Putting her finger to her lips, Ma shuts the door swiftly, then bolts the lock. My heart beats too fast. We get safety from being on the farmer's land, but it also costs us money. I wish we could afford to pay for things.

"Are you in there, Ma Hawker?" The farmer's voice is kind and warm, but I've seen lack of money turn people's words stone cold. "I know you are, so you may as well come out."

We try not to breathe.

"There's no excuse this time, I'm afraid," the farmer goes on. His fist bangs the door, and I squeal at the noise, then clamp my hand to my mouth. "Got mice in there, have you?" he asks.

Ma glares at me, and I curse myself in my head. Tom squeezes my hand.

"Hello?" Ma says feebly, then yawns loudly. She goes to the door and unlocks it. "Apologies. We were just taking a nap."

"At this time of morning?" the farmer says.

I go out to join her. "We didn't sleep well last night," I lie.

"Too many mice," Tom adds.

"I see," the farmer replies, but he's smirking at our used breakfast bowls. He doesn't believe us at all. "Well, you've been here a fortnight, and so far you've only paid for a week."

I can feel Ma shifting uncomfortably next to me. "We have money to collect today, Mr Meek," she says. "Someone bought one of our finest curios. I shall collect the money this afternoon, and you shall have your payment first thing tomorrow."

The farmer seems satisfied and tips his cap to us. Tom and I lock eyes. We both know what this means – we are moving on.

As soon as he is out of sight, Ma starts to pack. Quietly at first, in case the farmer comes back, but briskly.

"Can't we stay a bit longer, Ma?" Tom asks. "I like it here." He gazes sadly at the stepping stones he has created across the river.

"Get your things packed, please, Tom," Ma replies.

We know from experience that there is no point in arguing. We are wanderers, and the road ahead is our home.

"Come on, Tom, an adventure!" I say, so he remembers that is who we are and what we do.

He nods and sniffs the wind.

When night falls, we leave.

CHAPTER 3

I sit up front with Ma as we rattle our way down
moonlit lanes. Winnie pulls us along gently.
The feel of the road beneath us is familiar.
Bump. Judder. Shudder-ping. Jolt. The
repaired wheel holds up well, and I feel proud.

"Where are we going this time, Ma?" I ask.
Sometimes we follow the wind to discover a new
place. This time Ma consults a map and uses a
compass.

"The most wondrous place you have ever
seen, Lil," Ma says. The starlight is making her
silver. "London."

I feel excitement tickle my spine and nerves tingle my scalp. I've heard so many things about London – some of them good, some of them terrible, all of them interesting. To think I am going to see it for myself!

We pass fields, their grasses blue and purple in the night-time. Far-off villages crouch in darkness on the horizon. We bump and wind along. When we are far enough down the road, Ma and I sing to pass the travelling time.

Dawn arrives with the song of birds and scattering rabbits. The sun announces itself, golden across the land. It will be hot again today.

Weary, Ma pulls over for a rest. Tom comes out to join me, his eyes bleary. Ma takes his place in the bed.

"Are we stopping here instead of London, Lil?" Tom asks. He looks delighted. He loves the countryside more than anything.

"No," I say. "We are just resting for a short while."

I lead Winnie to a shady spot by a brook. When I return, Ma is fast asleep already. I take some bread for breakfast and Ma's small coin bag so that no one will steal it.

"Let's go for a stroll, Tom," I suggest. "Give Ma a bit of peace."

We wander to a field that smells of all our summers past. Long grasses ripple like the sea on a breezy day. There is an oak tree at its centre, so, naturally, we head for it. I am a lover of climbing, and Tom likes to think in the shade.

When we reach the oak, we sit and eat the bread and discuss the day. Then Tom lies back to observe the chinks of blue sky between the wavering green leaves.

I tuck my skirt into my knickers and begin to climb. Soon I am sitting on a high branch, with Tom's dappled face way below on the grass beneath the oak and jackdaws squawking around me.

I make a telescope of my hand to see in each direction.

There's a town, far off and smoky to the south. A bristling wood is to the west. Hills like boulders are to the east. The road behind us is north. I return my gaze to the south and see a boy hurrying across the field towards us. I climb down from the tree too fast, scraping my knee and making it bleed.

"What are you two doing?" the boy asks, his words abrupt.

"Nothing," I say. "What business is it of yours?" I forget my manners when people are rude.

He checks behind him as if he's being followed and replies, "Sorry, didn't mean to offend."

"Why are you rushing? Is someone chasing you?" I ask.

The boy narrows his eyes for a second, then, seeing I am smart, he nods.

"What have you done?" I ask. I don't want us to get involved in something bad.

"Oh, nothing," the boy says. "It's because I have treasure." He holds his battered leather case close to him.

"Treasure?" Tom gasps.

"Yes, but people want to steal it from me."

"Like pirates?" Tom asks.

"Exactly."

I want to know more. "What is it?" I say.

"Oh, just some curios I've collected on my travels around the world," the boy explains.

My jaw drops open. "Curios?"

"Yes," he says. "The most marvellous ones you've ever seen. I can give you a small peek if you like?"

The boy unclips the case and opens it secretively, but only for a moment. I catch a flash of something sparkling blue and a bone of some sort too before he snaps the case shut.

"An old bone and a bit of blue glass," I scoff as if I'm not interested.

"The greatest jewel your eye can ever behold and a bone from Egypt," the boy boasts.

Tom asks if he can see again, and the boy tells him that he's worried the sun will damage his ancient wonders.

"Dug from a pharaoh's pyramid," the boy whispers. "I'm so sorry to have to sell them. I'm sure you can imagine how people would gawp and wonder at them."

I *can* imagine it. This could save us. "Why are you selling them if they mean so much to you?" I ask.

A sick sister and an operation to pay for, he explains.

"Can we buy them?" I ask.

"I don't know." The boy scratches his chin. "Will you give them a good home?"

"Yes," Tom blurts out. "We are curio collectors."

"Well, I never," the boy replies, astonished. "What a coincidence."

I worry that this is a trap. But how can it be? We have never met this boy before. He knows nothing about us. "Perhaps we should go and ask our ma," I say.

"Yes, do that," he replies. "Where is she?"

I point the long way back to where our caravan is.

"It's just that I'm in such a hurry," the boy says. "I have another person waiting for them at that church there." He points to a church spire in the distance. "I'm already late. My sister is sickening fast."

I decide that we must take the risk and hand over Ma's money. Surely she will be proud of me? I feel a flutter of fear as he dashes off with our payment, but we have our treasure. My uncertainty grows as we get closer to the caravan.

"Ma," Tom calls out. He rushes forward to where she is winding up a clockwork toy tricycle to check it's still working. "We've got a surprise for you."

I carry the case behind him, and my heart drops into my boots when I see her expression. Ma does not look pleased at all.

"A boy sold them to us," I say. "He said that they were treasure." It sounds so unlikely suddenly. "Have a look at them, Ma."

"I've already seen them, Lil," Ma says.

I'm confused.

"He wanted to sell them to me," she explains.

Shocked, I drop the case.

"He saw our collection of curios and tried to get rid of this junk," Ma says. She throws the case open and shakes her head. There are broken bits of a music box and a moth-eaten stuffed bird. The sparkle was a cracked mirror reflecting the sky and the bone from a rabbit and fit only for a dog.

"Well, at least this will come in useful," Ma says, and takes out a big clam shell with strange markings on it. She uses it to bung a

hole in one of our storage cases, then stomps
off, leaving us devastated.

CHAPTER 4

We don't speak to each other as we travel on, and Tom and I sit indoors sulking. But eventually we feel the road beneath us become less bumpy, and we're too curious not to look.

We open the top of the caravan door and see the fields giving way to tall buildings and gaslights. The pavements are lined with all sorts of people going about their business. Women in bonnets carry babies. Men read newspapers in groups. I lick my lips as we pass a confectioner's – its jars of sweets gleam deliciously in the window. A horse-drawn omnibus passes, and Tom whoops with joy.

This must be London! We clamber out as soon as the caravan comes to a halt, unable to ignore our excitement.

"This is Highgate," Ma Hawker tells us as we gawp at everything around us. "And that's the whole of London before you."

We can see roofs stretching away into the distance. Thousands of chimneys choke up smoke. The dome of a huge cathedral looks impressive even from here. The sound of all the busy streets rises up towards us, and our mouths fall open as we take in the size of it all.

We are overawed and spend a long time drinking it in. Then we remember that we are all still cross with each other. We Hawkers don't let an argument go to waste. Heavy clouds hang still in the sky, and the heat is suffocating. Tom glares at me for getting him into trouble, and Ma doesn't look at me at all. My skin burns with the unfairness of it.

We have pulled up next to a market, and Ma blows out her cheeks. "Set out the curios, Lil," she says, and nods at me. I think it is her attempt at forgiveness.

I unhook the clasps that hold the storage cases in place – hinged shelves on the outside of the caravan. I made them myself, so I know how they fold, slot and bolt. When there's no space to keep things inside, you have to put them outside.

I check that none of our curios are damaged from the trip. A few of them have fallen over but not broken. The shell is still wedged into the hole, a sore reminder of my mistake. I try my best not to look at it.

"Right then, you two." Ma wipes dirt from our faces. "We are going to put on a show!"

I fetch my little drum, and Tom dusts off the top hat we keep for these occasions.

Ma holds up an umbrella like it's a sword and hollers, "Welcome to the fantastical cabinet of curiosities!"

I skip about, trying to drum up a crowd. "There is nothing else like it in the whole wide world!" I bellow. "Come, be astonished. Be mesmerised by our marvels!"

A few people stop to watch. Tom juggles some glass eyes, and I dance and bang my drum.

"Behold, our wonders!" Ma calls as she shows a skeleton playing a violin.

I slip into the crowd, pushing one of the ladies forward to try on a snakeskin crown complete with venomous fangs. Ma made it out of an old piece of leather and some of her own teeth. It's fairly convincing, and people will believe anything these days.

That's modern life for you. People are just looking for quick entertainment, surprises and shocks. Some of them put coins in the upturned hat Tom is holding now; others deliberately move away as he approaches.

We keep most of the crowd interested for a while with our organs and specimens. But as soon as Ma holds up a narwhal tusk, telling them it's a unicorn's horn, we lose them in a wave of disinterest and a rumble of thunder.

We pack away. We've got it down to an art, so it takes us less than three minutes. Fold up shelves on hinges, buckle chests, snap clasps into place, tie fraying ropes. Everything is stowed away just before the first fat raindrops begin to fall.

It's been a successful show, and we've made a good amount of money. But we usually make more from selling the curios to rich idiots than from shows. Anyway, it's enough for Ma to go off to purchase food.

Me and Tom wait hungrily. We sit under Ma's umbrella and take in all the sights. A car passes, splashing people as it drives into puddles, which causes a lot of excitement.

Mourners pass too, on their way to Highgate Cemetery. Their carriages glisten with the heavily falling rain. The black feather plumes the horses wear on their heads droop and sag as they get soaked. Tom and I plan our funerals and hope they'll be extravagant and expensive.

The rain stops as suddenly as it began, and Tom shakes the umbrella all over me. I go to chase him, but I'm stopped by a tap on my shoulder.

"Excuse me," says a maid. She's not much older than me but very prim and proper in her manners.

"What for?" Tom elbows me, and I laugh.

"I'd like to buy your scrimshaw, please," the maid says.

I don't know what she's talking about, but I hear that she wants to buy something, and I want an opportunity to make up for my recent mistake.

"What's a scrimshaw?" Tom asks, and I'm glad he does so I don't have to.

"That shell, there."

The maid points to the big clam shell Ma has used to fill the hole in the storage case. The one from the worthless collection of junk I paid for. I give Tom a side-eye so that he doesn't tell her it's worth nothing.

"Oh, that shell!" I exclaim, pressing my hands to my heart. "That is a very precious item indeed, isn't it, Tom?"

He smiles as he catches on to my plan.

"Oh, very important, Lily," Tom confirms.

"How much?" the maid asks wearily.

I feel ashamed of myself, but we need the money desperately. I pop the shell out from the hole. It's quite big and has an engraving on it. I don't know what the carvings are supposed to be. It's interesting, but money is more important.

"A sixpence," I say to start our bargaining high.

"I don't have that much money." The maid looks sad. "Can I pay you in instalments?"

"I'm afraid not," I reply firmly. "We'll be on the road again soon."

"We are wanderers, you see," Tom adds.

"How wonderful," the maid says, smiling dreamily. "To be free to roam the world. You must have such adventures."

I warm to her now. "We do," I confirm proudly.

"One day I shall travel the world and see great things just as you do," the maid says.

I like this girl. If I can sell this shell, perhaps Ma will forgive me for buying the junk.

"You can have it for threepence," I say. "It's expensive because it's unique."

The maid opens her purse to see if she has enough, then checks behind her as if she is worried someone is about to steal it from her. She catches sight of a fine gentleman approaching and snaps the purse shut again, a look of fear crossing her face.

She moves closer to me and whispers, "Please keep it for me. It's very important." She pleads desperately, and her eyes glisten with tears. This shell means so much to her.

"I will," I promise, solemnly crossing my heart.

"Keep it safe for me. I'll come back," the maid says as she dashes off.

"Wait!" I call after her, but she ignores me.

"That was odd behaviour," I say to Tom.

The only thing I can see that might have frightened the maid is the gentleman who has now come right up to our caravan. He stares at us, twirling his moustache with his fingertips. Then he looks down at the scrimshaw shell I'm still holding.

The gentleman smiles at me, but something about his manner makes me feel uneasy. Why was the maid so scared of him?

I pretend not to notice him as I put the shell into the pocket of my pinafore and busy myself with the storage cases. After a moment, the gentleman walks away.

"Come on, Tom," I say, yanking him by the arm. "We need that money."

We race after the maid, the shell bouncing about in my pocket. We're just in time to see her disappear through an arched gate in a high wall.

"We've lost her," says Tom.

Past the bars of the gate is a very rich-looking house. This must be where the maid works.

"Don't worry, Tom," I say. "We won't give up. We'll come back."

Taking the shell from my pocket, I examine the carvings again. I wonder why the maid wants it so much and why that fine gentleman scared her away.

CHAPTER 5

We are tired but pleased with today's takings. Ma has counted up the money twice. The sound of the ha'pennies and farthings as she handles them is music to our ears.

Ma's face gleams in the candlelight and we sit back, hands clasped over our full stomachs. For once, we have eaten well.

I've shared some of my supper with the crows who pecked about outside. Then I watched them fly off towards the huge cemetery, which must be where they live.

Summer storm rain drums on the caravan roof again, and we are squashed together like peas in a pod.

"What a marvellous place Highgate is," I say, winking at Tom as we put our plan into action. We want to convince Ma to stay here so we can find that maid and sell her the shell. We've decided not to tell Ma the truth because we don't want to get her hopes up. I nod at Tom to get him to answer.

"It is my very favourite place I have ever been," he agrees, then bites his lip because he has overdone it a bit.

"And the centre of London will be even better," Ma joins in.

"It will be," I say, thinking quickly. "It's just that there are so many rich people here. When Tom and I went for a walk, we saw huge houses. Velvet drapes at the windows, chandeliers inside."

41

"And new people arrive every day," says Tom.

I smile at him. It's a good point. There are so many visitors coming to Highgate to visit the cemetery. We've watched crowds of people arriving. They want to wander amongst the graves of famous people and admire the architecture. Death is very fashionable these days. It's good for us too as there's a lot of passing trade.

We feel the shift in Ma's concentration as her counting slows. We can almost hear the cogs of her brain working.

"It's a shame we have to move on so fast," I add. "Perhaps we can come back this way one day." Then I let the thought linger with Ma, signalling to Tom to talk about something else, and we chatter about a train he saw.

"I've made a decision," Ma announces. "We are going to stay here a couple of nights."

We pretend to be surprised by Ma's news.

"My knees are playing up," she says, as if to explain her decision.

Ma will never admit her worries about money.

We are thrilled, but we don't let it show in case Ma gets suspicious. If we are staying, we can go and find that maid again.

I squeeze Tom tight with excitement, then settle down to sleep.

*

I wake as the town clock strikes midnight, the chimes ringing out loudly into the heat. Wait! There is another noise. My ears struggle in the darkness to identify it. Small and scratching. A rat? Perhaps Ma has gone outside to relieve herself?

No, I can hear her soft snores. Tom is next to me, wriggling in his dreams.

I try to open my ears to listen harder. My heart is in my mouth. Am I imagining it? There's a creak as the door opens a little, making me scream. Ma is up like a bolt of lightning. There is nothing wrong with her knees when she knows there might be trouble.

"What do you want?" Ma shouts, catching hold of the figure. I grab our biggest pan to defend us if I need to.

"Forgive me, dear lady," the man says, struggling to be free of her grip. "I saw your show earlier. I'm interested in your curios, is all. Fascinated, in fact."

"Funny time of night to be wanting to look at them," I snarl.

"Correct, dear girl." The man's voice slithers around us. "I'm afraid I'm rather a night owl.

I've been experimenting with photography to see if I can get good images in the dark. My sincere apologies for causing any alarm."

"Where is your camera?" I ask.

"I left it with a friend," the gentleman replies.

A likely story.

"Why did you try to break in?" I say. I'm not ready to let it go.

"I thought I heard soft singing. I wanted to peek quietly to see if you were still awake."

Ma knows that she sings sometimes in her sleep, and she removes her grip from him. I don't put the pan down. I know there wasn't any singing. Tom lights a candle, and we gasp as we see the man's face. It's the gentleman who scared the maid away.

"Wait a minute. I recognise you," Ma says,
excited. She picks up a newspaper that's shared
around the market traders. "I knew it," she
says, reading the headline from the paper.
"Horatio Pinch to be honoured."

The man looks annoyed but covers it quickly
with a false smile.

Ma continues to read the article. "Horatio Pinch is to collect an award for his services to botany at Kew Gardens. Mr Pinch has discovered and brought back plants from all over the world."

She stops here, her eyes shining. There is nothing Ma likes more than someone she might be able to convince to take her around the globe.

"It's true," says the gentleman. "I am Horatio Pinch. At your service, madam."

He bows, knocking over our ship in a bottle which had been balanced on Ma's shelf of favourite things. Ma touches it wistfully every day as she dreams of sailing the waves.

We are horrified, but Ma lets the bottle roll without reaction.

"As luck would have it, we are staying here for a few days," she says, thrilled at his fame and spying the golden chain to his pocket watch. "We are showing our curios to everyone. Marvellous things they are."

"Wonderful news, dear lady," Pinch says, taking Ma's hand and kissing it.

Wise and old as Ma is, she loves a bit of flattery. She giggles, and I try not to be sick.

"I'm particularly interested in things from overseas. Shells and the like," Pinch says.

Tom and I exchange glances, thinking of the shell that the maid wanted to buy.

"We have lots of those, Mr Pinch," says Ma.

"Horatio, please," the gentleman insists.

"We'll polish up our best overseas curios for you tomorrow, Horatio," Ma tells him.

"Can I see them now?" he asks.

"I really would rather you return. Perhaps we could take a sunset stroll." Ma flutters her eyelids.

"Until tomorrow then," Pinch says. He tries to turn, but there's no room, so he shuffles out of the caravan sideways like a crab.

"Well, that was a bit of excitement," Ma says. She fastens the door and blows out the candle to hide the glow of her cheeks.

We get back into bed and wait to hear Ma's snores. When they come, I grab my pinafore from a hook inside the door and poke Tom's arm. We creep outside, checking that Pinch has gone, and I take the shell out from the pocket of my pinafore.

We examine the scrimshaw as best we can in the flame of the streetlamps. There's a circle on it and some lines too, but we can't make out what they are supposed to be. Something tells me they are more important than just a pretty pattern. I think they are supposed to show us something. But what?

"He's after this, isn't he?" Tom asks.

"He is," I say. "But I don't know why." I rack my brains. The shell is big, yes, and pretty to the eye. But is it something worth trying to steal in the middle of the night? The maid wanted this too. And to pay good money for it. What secret does it hold?

Tom rubs his finger over the grooves. "What are they, Lil?" he asks me.

"I'm not sure, Tom. But we are going to find out."

CHAPTER 6

The morning comes. We are tired from our
disturbed sleep but also excited by the prospect
of our investigation. Before the newspaper gets
passed on to another trader, I cut the piece
about Horatio Pinch out with Ma's dressmaking
scissors and put it in my pocket.

We work hard, performing another three
shows back to back. Ma is delighted by the
money we've made in collections and from sales
to the rich people of Highgate. An ammonite
fossil, a dried-up starfish and a stuffed cat have
all been sold today.

Pinch shows up as the third show ends, and Ma shoos us away, much to our delight.

We sneakily take the shell and leave Pinch searching through the curios with Ma.

We might end up selling the scrimshaw to him, but me and Tom don't like Pinch much. There's something slimy about him and the way he was sneaking about in the night.

Also, I promised the maid she could have the shell, and I always keep my promises when I can.

We should tell Ma, but if we do, she'll sell it to Pinch. She is smitten with him, and he would pay a better price, I'm certain.

"Come on, Tom," I say.

We run all the way to the gate where the maid disappeared. But then we can't think of an excuse for going into the garden and disturbing the people who own the house.

"We'll just have to wait," Tom grumbles, sinking down to a crouch as he feels the adventure slipping through our fingers.

Tom's glumness spurs me into action. "I'm going to climb this wall to see if I can see her," I tell him. "You be lookout."

This is a quiet leafy street, but people do pass us occasionally. "What if we get caught, Lil?" Tom asks.

"I'll only be a minute," I say, and start to shin up the wall. It is high, but the ivy growing on it helps me to grip on, and I am a very good climber.

Soon I can peer over the top of the wall. We are in luck. The maid is in the kitchen garden. She's talking to the flowers. It's a peculiar thing to do, but I've seen much stranger things on our travels.

"Hello there," I call to the maid, and she yells out, startled.

I climb a bit higher so that my face shows over the wall. "It's me," I say. "You wanted to buy a shell from me yesterday."

The maid checks that no one is watching from the house and motions for me to get down. I do and go to the gate with Tom. Soon we see the maid on the other side of the iron bars. She lets us in.

"Quietly," she says, and beckons us to follow. The maid leads the way to a kitchen entrance, then along a passageway and up the servants' stairs to an attic.

She ushers us into a bedroom and shuts the door. My mouth falls open. The room is filled with shells and bones all engraved with different markings. There must be at least thirty here. On the windowsill. On shelves. Under the bed.

"What's this?" Tom asks as he holds up a curved bone the length of his hand.

"It's a whale's tooth," the maid tells him. She's listening at the door to make sure we weren't followed. Tom's eyes widen to the size of saucers.

"You must really like scrimshaw," I say.

"I do." The maid nods. "Here's your money."

"It's twice as much now for the trouble we've been to," I say. I feel mean, but I know how to bargain.

The maid scowls, then scrabbles around trying to find more coins.

Curiosity gets the better of me. "What is so special about this one?" I ask. Some of the others she has seem far more beautiful to look at.

"It's a secret," the maid says.

"I'm good at keeping secrets," Tom says solemnly.

"I'm looking for a specific scrimshaw," the maid tells us. "It's mine, and it's important to me."

"Did someone steal it from you?" I ask.

The maid nods.

"People stole stuff from us lots of times, didn't they, Lil?" Tom says.

"Then you'll understand," the maid says, looking us up and down. "Can I trust you?"

We promise.

"My name is Flora Meriweather," she says. "My mother was Henrietta Meriweather. She engraved a scrimshaw for me before she died." It seems to hurt the maid to speak – like the sadness is too much for her.

"My mother left me at the foundling hospital when she contracted malaria – it's a disease you get from mosquito bites in hot countries. She knew she wouldn't recover. I was only a baby. She left the scrimshaw with me and told one of the people there that one day it would tell me everything I needed to know. But there was a robbery, and the scrimshaw was one of the things that was stolen."

Flora strikes a match and raises the wick on an oil lamp, then draws the curtains. The room springs to life. The engravings of all the scrimshaws glow. There are large ships sailing on the walls in the wavering light. Eagles,

symbols and strange creatures I've never seen before dance and soar around the room.

I understand how much it would hurt to have something so wonderful stolen from you. "They are beautiful," I say.

Flora looks at me hopefully.

"You can have it for twopence," I tell her. It's the right thing to do. Flora doesn't have a lot of money, that much is obvious.

I take the scrimshaw from my pocket and give it to her, praying it is the one she has been seeking. She puts it next to the oil lamp. It throws a pattern onto the wall to join the others. The engravings are too delicate to see with the naked eye but are now made bigger and sharper. There, clear as day, are the initials H.M.

Flora sinks to the floor. "It's the one."

We kneel next to her and feel the moment with our hearts. When Flora is ready, she speaks.

"My mother was a botanist and a biologist. A person who worked with plants. She studied them and their uses. She travelled the whole world to discover them. Climbed the most dangerous cliffs and braved the deepest jungles. She went where no one else dared. Many of the plants my mother found have medicinal properties which have helped cure terrible illnesses."

We are impressed.

"The woman at the foundling hospital told me all about her," Flora goes on. "My mother left me this scrimshaw for a reason. It must lead to something important."

We are lost in thought.

"And now a strange man is following me everywhere and has asked me about my scrimshaw collection," Flora says.

"Horatio Pinch," Tom blurts out. "He tried to get into our caravan last night."

Flora is astonished.

"Pinch is going to be given an award at Kew Gardens for his services to botany tomorrow," I tell her, and take the newspaper cutting from my pocket. "We found this."

"Well, this explains everything," Flora replies. The paper shakes in her hands. "It says he travelled the world with my mother. Don't you see?"

We shake our heads.

"She found these plants," Flora says. "Pinch is trying to steal her discoveries and claim them as his own. I'm sure of it."

"What a villain! I hated him on sight," I say.

"We just need to work out what the picture on the scrimshaw means," says Flora.

We all stare at it till our eyes water. It is a circle with lines leading out from it. Flora paces the floor and we copy her, bumping into each other several times.

"Could it be a merry-go-round?" I say. "Or the large wheel of a penny farthing?" It's all I can think of.

Excited, Tom jumps onto the bed, bouncing its springs. "Is it Stonehenge?" he asks. "We passed there once on our way to Devon."

"Oh!" Flora says. She's suddenly as still as a statue. "I know what it is. It's a map." She points at the pattern. "I know this place too well. My mother and father are buried there. It's Highgate Cemetery."

Flora points out the bits of the cemetery she recognises – the Egyptian Avenue, the Circle of Lebanon.

"I have to find out where the map leads," she says, her voice shaking with excitement. "Look. Where she's put her initials. Right

in the centre. I think it means that she has hidden something there."

This sounds like an adventure, and Tom and I offer to help. We make a plan to sneak back to meet Flora tonight when darkness falls, and then we'll go with her to the cemetery. Surely together we can solve the mystery and find whatever Flora's mother has left for her?

Flora gives us a different scrimshaw in case Horatio Pinch comes back to our caravan looking for it. She hides her mother's one safely under her bed. We sneak downstairs and out of the garden.

In the street we watch as a funeral procession passes – men in black suits and women wailing, their faces covered by black lace.

When we get back to our caravan, Ma is in a dark mood because Horatio Pinch flew into a rage when she couldn't produce the scrimshaw shell. Ma doesn't much care where we've been as she's too wrapped up in herself. But soon she calls me over, and I know what's coming before she opens her mouth.

"It's time to move on, Lil. We'll stay tonight and set out first thing."

We won't be able to change Ma's mind again. We have got to help Flora to solve the mystery of the scrimshaw map tonight.

CHAPTER 7

It stays light late because of the time of year. We wait an age as Ma gossips with a flower seller and shares sips from her hip flask. This is good news for us. She sleeps extremely soundly after brandy.

Eventually, darkness gathers, and Ma reels to her chair. It is safe to leave. We put a blanket over Winnie, then hurry off.

By the time we get to Flora's house, we are out of breath. The street is in darkness as we wait for Flora. Soon, she creeps out and our quest begins. Pinch intends to pick up his award tomorrow, so we don't have much time.

Flora leads the way, and we follow as quietly as we can.

In the day I am not very afraid of ghouls and spectres and ghosts. But the cemetery is so different at night. As we enter, crosses and tombs loom out of the darkness, but it's not just the dangers of the dead we need to worry about. Grave robbers and doctors who want corpses for scientific experiments are known to wander here at night. I think they would be very unhappy to find three young people spoiling their fun.

"Ouch," I say as Tom bumps into me yet again because he's following so closely.

"I'm scared, Lil," he says.

I want to call him a baby, but I'm frightened too.

"We'll stick together," Flora whispers.

I follow her closely between headstones. The cold slinks into my skirts, making me think of skeletal fingers reaching out to grab me.

"This way," Flora says. She has a tiny lamp. The light from it barely reaches her face. We follow that little glow hopefully, stumbling over tree roots and potholes.

"Ouch," I say. Tom has bumped into me again. As I turn, I'm sure I see another light behind us. It disappears immediately. Shivers rattle my spine. Was it my eyes playing tricks on me? There, again, is a glimmer. Tom has seen it too.

"Lil," he says.

"I know," I reply, and grab Flora's arm. "There's someone else here."

She pulls us down to crouch behind a crypt and hides the light of her lamp with her hands. We hold our breath.

Footsteps.

Gripping each other, we wait for whoever or *whatever* it is to go away.

"There's no point in hiding, I'm afraid," says a voice that's snakelike and familiar. "I know you are there. I have a pistol, and I'm not afraid to shoot."

We help each other to stand on shaky legs and face our enemy.

"Horatio Pinch!" The words are out of my mouth before I can stop them.

"The very same," he replies. His face is devilish in the flickering lamplight. "And now I'll take that scrimshaw if you please."

He puts his hand out for it.

"It's here," I say, quickly pulling out the replacement scrimshaw Flora gave me earlier. I'd forgotten all about it till this moment.

"Thank you." He snatches the shell. The markings on it show a triangle and a cat. "What does it mean?" he asks, pointing the pistol at us.

"We don't know," Flora tells him truthfully.

"Are you going to kill us?" Tom asks. He's standing in front of me so that he will be shot first. I pull him back so that the three of us stand side by side.

"We can't help you now, Mr Pinch," I say. His name tastes foul in my mouth. "So we'll be on our way."

Pinch isn't listening to me but is staring at the shell, trying to understand the image. "It's a pyramid," he says, thrilled. "Aha! The Egyptian Avenue, of course. It's just over there."

I gasp, pretending to be shocked by his cleverness.

"You fools couldn't work that out? So close and yet so far." Pinch scoffs with laughter at us. "I, Horatio Pinch, will have what is due to me."

He rushes off.

"You're the clever one, Lil," Tom says proudly. "That was close."

"Come on," I say. I'm pleased that we have managed to keep the real scrimshaw hidden from Pinch's grasping hands, but I know that he'll be back.

CHAPTER 8

We have been searching in the cemetery for hours now. Tom is tired and moans every two minutes. I am cold and miserable. Flora seems close to despair. Grey ghostly light starts to gather, making the shapes of the graveyard clearer by the second. Crows croak the morning in. The day is beginning, and time is running out.

"What shall we do?" Tom asks. He kicks a gravestone in frustration, then rubs it as an apology. Flora sits down on a verge and shakes her head. I gently take the scrimshaw from her and hold it up to the light in the hope of noticing something new. Without warning, a crow caws then swoops down and steals it from my hand with its beak, taking it up into the branches of a huge tree.

"No," Flora gasps, her voice croaking like the bird's. "Bring it back."

"Wait," I say, and close my eyes so I can think more clearly. "Crows are clever. Perhaps it is trying to tell us something."

"What do you mean?" Flora says. She comes and stands next to me.

"Didn't you say your mother loved plants?" I ask.

"Yes," Flora confirms. "But this isn't the time for me to give you a lesson on trees."

"And didn't you say she climbed to places where no one else dared go?" I continue, excited now.

"Oh," Flora says, understanding what I mean now.

We look up at the tree.

"The Cedar of Lebanon," she says.

"What are you two burbling on about?" Tom asks, coming to join us.

"Don't you see, Tom?" Flora goes on. "My mother loved plants. In a place of dead things, she would always seek out the living. And here on the scrimshaw, this carving in the circle must be a tree, and look around us!"

We realise that this tree is right in the centre of a circle of tombs.

Tom grasps what Flora is getting at. "You think she hid something there?"

We all jump as there is a sudden yelling sound. It must be Horatio Pinch, frustrated by his pointless search. We climb over the tombs which have been built around the tree, trying to get to its trunk.

"Quick," Tom says.

Flora points up.

Of course. "The perfect hiding place," I say.

It's easy to get my first foothold, and soon I am high up. I scan the graveyard and spot Pinch. He's pacing between the tombs, and even from here I can tell that he is furious.

Other people are appearing too. There are those who tend the graveyard, keeping it tidy. Early mourners arriving. A man with a rake stops to talk to Pinch, and he is stuck there making polite conversation.

I climb further. Huge branches strike out in all directions, but I think that Flora's mother would have kept to the centre. The trunk of

the tree is less likely to be broken by a strong
wind or damaged very much if it is hit by
lightning. I press my ear to the bark and listen.
I'm hoping the cedar will tell me its secrets.
Something is hidden here. I know it is.

Further up, there's a hole in the trunk. I gently put my hand in and check that there isn't a bird or any other animal living in there. Then I feel around properly.

Bravely, I push my arm in further so that I'm up to my elbow. My fingertips feel something strange. Not the soft wood of the inside, or the warm stickiness of sap, but something smooth. I dislodge it from its place and wriggle it towards me with my fingers. It doesn't come easily, but I keep coaxing.

Way below I can hear Flora telling someone that she is here to visit her mother's and father's graves. Tom is peering up worriedly. In the distance, I see Pinch leave. He must be going to get his award.

I can't rush for fear of breaking the object, whatever it is. I keep teasing it towards me. Finally, I ease it out of the hole.

It's a leather-bound journal. I blow dirt from the cover and rub small spores of mould away. Now I can see H.M. embossed on it in gold. My heart hammers inside my chest. Tucking the journal into my dress, I shimmy down again, checking that the coast is clear before I finally drop to land near Tom and Flora.

"I found this." I give it to Flora, who examines the cover as if she can't believe her eyes.

She opens it and turns the pages. It has lots of writing and drawings of flowers.

"My mother's diary," Flora says. "This will prove it was she who made all those discoveries." She bursts into tears.

"Now we must get to Kew," I urge her. "We haven't a second to lose."

CHAPTER 9

"Lil. Tom," says Ma. "Where have you been?"

She is livid. I don't blame her. She can tell from our faces that something important has happened.

"What is it?" Ma goes on. "Are you in trouble? Are you well? Who is this?"

"We're fine, Ma," I say. "This is Flora." I push Flora forward so quickly she almost bumps into Ma.

"Flora Meriweather, madam," Flora says. "And these two have changed my life."

Ma listens to us telling her the story of everything that has happened while a hundred different expressions cross her face. She admires the beautiful drawings in the diary, shaking her head in wonder.

"And the award is being given at Kew at noon today." Flora shows her the newspaper cutting. "We have to get there before it starts."

"Then there's no time to lose," Ma says. She studies a map and blows her cheeks out. "It's near on nine miles, I'd say."

Outside, Winnie neighs.

"That's my girl," Ma says, beaming.

We all cram in next to each other and set off. People leap out of the way as we go past.

"Sorry!" I yell. "It's a matter of adventure."

At first, it's glorious fun. But all too soon the worry sets in that we won't make it in time. Flora grips my arm, her knuckles white. Winnie slows, and soon the familiar bump, judder, shudder-ping, jolt is joined by another noise, and it isn't good.

There's a sudden cracking sound, and the wheel I'd repaired rolls off. The caravan tips sidewards so violently I have to grab Tom to stop him from falling.

"We'll have to run," I say, jumping down and helping Flora down too.

"I'll stay with Winnie," Ma says. "Take this with you."

She gives us the map and shows us the direction. "Good luck."

We hug her briefly, then run as if our lives depend on it – which for Flora is the truth.

CHAPTER 10

We arrive at Kew Gardens, panting for breath.
It has taken us hours to get here, and I'm
worried we are too late. There are lots of
people milling about. They are all dressed
in fine clothes. Top hats and suits. Women
wear beautiful dresses that try to outshine the
flowers.

We keep going. These people are all posh.
Flora might be able to slip amongst them in her
maid's uniform, but our clothes are scruffy and
we are sweaty. Because of this we duck behind
bushes and trees whenever people pass. We
don't want to draw attention to ourselves or,

even more disastrous, have Pinch spot us before we try to put things right.

Crowds stream into a huge glass building. Thousands of window panes reflect the sun. Brass-band music pours out. A woman spots us peeking from behind a clump of ferns and scowls at us. I stand up to glare at her. It's a mistake.

A gardener approaches us. "What are you doing here?" they ask.

"We are going in there." Tom points at the glass building.

"The Temperate House?" the gardener says. "I don't think you are dressed for a party, young man."

"Oh my. What a beauty," Flora says, delighted by the flower the gardener carries. "*Cymbidium*. Also known as a boat orchid. Most commonly found in the Himalayas."

"You certainly know your flowers." The gardener is impressed.

"I thought all gardeners were men, but you're a woman," Tom says, stating the obvious.

"I am." The gardener laughs. "And one of the very first women to work here."

"That must be the most glorious job in the whole wide world," Flora says, smiling.

"It's certainly interesting." The gardener seems to be softening towards us, but then she says, "Now, I think you should be on your way."

The music reaches a crescendo. Through the glass we see more posh people getting up onto a platform. Horatio Pinch is there, smiling like the cat who got the cream.

"We have to get in," I plead.

"Please," Flora begs. Then the whole story of her mother pours out in a mixed-up order, but we fill in the gaps for it to make sense.

"So that man is trying to take the credit for your mother's discoveries?" the gardener asks.

"He is," Flora says. She's on the verge of tears.

I show the gardener the diary, and she is astounded by its contents.

"Your mother found all those exotic plants, and these are her drawings in there?" the gardener asks.

"She did and they are."

"Then she was quite a woman."

I look at the pride on Flora's face and burst into tears. I wasn't expecting to feel so emotional. Flora hooks her arm into mine.

"And that man in there is trying to claim that it is all his work," the gardener says.

We nod. Inside the Temperate House, the crowd applauds. A woman in a white-feathered hat is making a speech and holding an award. Pinch is standing next to her, attempting to look modest.

"Well, we can't let him get away with that now, can we?" the gardener says, and marches ahead of us.

Inside, people are sitting listening and fanning themselves, or standing around with champagne glasses in their hands.

"Stop, thief!" I shout without thinking. Even I am surprised. Flora and Tom start shouting too.

Every head turns to look at us. The woman in the feathered hat screeches like a parrot, as do some of the other ladies. We cause quite the commotion.

"Take these urchins out, please," the woman in the feathered hat orders. Some burly men begin making their way through the crowd towards us.

"You will not make them leave," the gardener says. She holds up the rake she has been working with as a weapon and makes a path for us through the crowd. People fall aside like autumn leaves.

"What is going on?" Pinch says, outraged. His face is poppy-red. Spittle flies from his lips.

"I'm getting these three to the front so they can tell their story," the gardener shouts back.

"And claim what is rightfully ours!" I shout. "Hers," I correct myself, pushing Flora forward.

It is very satisfying to see the horror on Pinch's face.

"Get them out of here!" he shrieks. His voice is so high-pitched that one of the champagne glasses shatters.

"Over my dead body," the gardener says.

"And mine," Tom adds, picking up a potted plant as if he's going to throw it.

"That's enough," the woman in the feathered hat says. She is clearly important because everyone goes quiet.

"But ..." Pinch stutters.

"Enough, I said."

Pinch seethes with anger but is too afraid to continue.

"Explain yourselves, please," the woman commands us. "And put that down."

Tom puts the plant down, and Flora explains. Slowly and powerfully. She passes the diary over and some people examine it. Murmurs ripple through the crowd. It seems some of them knew Flora's mother. Some of them don't like Horatio Pinch.

When Flora gets to the end of the story, all eyes are on Pinch.

"Is this true?" the woman demands.

"No. Absolutely not," Pinch says. "You would rather take the word of this scraggle of children and this common man than mine?"

"I am no man," the gardener states proudly. "And these children have more heart and talent and charm in their little toes than you have in your whole body."

Some of the crowd laugh at this. A few of them clap. Pinch must feel the tide turning against him, and he tries to make his escape. His way is blocked. He puts his hand into his pocket and pulls out a pistol, aiming it at us.

"Get out of my way or I'll shoot," Pinch warns.

"It seems I'm not the only troublesome woman here," the gardener says, pointing to where two more women gardeners are approaching Pinch from behind so he doesn't see them. One of them knocks his feet away with a spade, making him drop the pistol and fall off the stage into a wheelbarrow.

I grab the pistol and point it at him, my hand shaking. There is a huge cheer from everyone, and two policemen enter and put Pinch in handcuffs. He is wheeled out, and Flora is beckoned up onto the stage.

"I believe this is yours," the woman in the hat says, giving Flora the award. We all cheer so loudly I'm surprised that the whole place doesn't explode.

CHAPTER 11

We sit on deckchairs in the sun. Ma Hawker has arrived, having fixed the caravan wheel herself, and is telling her version of events to anyone who'll listen. Winnie has been taken to a nearby stables to rest. Tom and I are eating ice creams awarded to us for our bravery by the gardeners.

Flora comes rushing over. "You'll never believe it," she says. "I've been offered a home here in Kew."

"To work as a maid?" I say excitedly.

"Better. To become an apprentice in the gardens and continue my mother's work."

The gardener who helped us smiles from where she is tending roses, and Flora waves to her. "Can you believe it?" Flora says.

I can. I take her hand, and she doesn't mind that mine is sticky with ice cream.

"They are going to hold a display of my scrimshaws here too," Flora adds, "along with their art collection, and give any proceeds to the foundling hospital."

"It couldn't be more perfect," I sigh.

"This one is for you," Flora says. "For your curio collection." She gives us the scrimshaw her mother had carved. I try to refuse, but Flora insists. I put it in my pocket, knowing we'll be friends for ever.

Tom makes shapes of the clouds with his finger, and I smell the heady perfume of flowers on the air. It's mixed with the sweet scent of something else. We rest for a while, happy in our spot in the sun.

Ma comes over with pound notes in her hand. "We've been given a reward for helping to find the lost diary," she explains. "It belongs to you two really."

"You keep it, Ma." I smile, knowing we'll be well looked after.

"Yes, keep it," Tom says. "But I should like another ice." He licks the last drips from his wrist.

Ma goes to get some, and we lie back lazily. I try again to make out what is causing that sweet smell. After a while, Ma returns with a lot of excitement and a complete lack of ice cream.

"You'll never guess what I've just seen," she says. "An exhibition of photographs of Paris. The building of the Eiffel Tower. Boats trips in the sewers and along the River Seine. Artists painting in the streets. So many fine people. Imagine the curios we could find there! We could sail across the sea and make our fortune." Ma's eyes glow.

And now I know what the aroma on the air is. It's the sweet smell of adventure.

Ma goes to get Winnie, and we say our goodbyes to Flora.

"Can't you stay?" she pleads.

"We can't." Tom shakes his head. "We are wanderers."

"We are more than that, Tom," I say, my gaze on the horizon now that this adventure is over. "We are the curio collectors."